First American edition 1993
Macmillan Publishing Company is part of the
Maxwell Communication Group of Companies.
Macmillan Publishing Company
866 Third Avenue, New York, NY 10022
First published in 1992 by Julia MacRae, an imprint of
Random Century Ltd., London, England.
Printed in Hong Kong

10 9 8 7 6 5 4 3 2 1

ISBN 0-02-754700-0

My Wicked Stepmother

NORMAN LEACH
Illustrated by JANE BROWNE

MACMILLAN PUBLISHING COMPANY NEW YORK

MAXWELL MACMILLAN INTERNATIONAL
NEW YORK OXFORD SINGAPORE SYDNEY

My name is Tom. I live with my dad.
We were happy together. . . .

But now I have a wicked stepmother.
She is a witch. I hate her. My dad thinks he loves her.
She put a spell on him and he thinks she is young and beautiful, but
I know she is middle-aged and ugly and a horrible witch.

My Dad gave me a new Robin Hood outfit.
It has a green tunic and a hat and a bow and arrow.

I went to show my friend Jack.
He said, "So what? I got one of
those last year."

I went to show my friend David. He said,
"Bows and arrows are boring!
I've got a laser gun."

I was fed up. I went back home.
The wicked stepmother said, "Tom, you look great
in that Robin Hood suit. Let me see you shoot
your bow and arrow."

But I didn't, because I'm not nice to wicked stepmothers.

My Dad gave me a Superman cape made with real silk! I put it on.

I went to show my friend David
He said, "So what? I got one of
those last year."

I went to show my friend Jack.
He said, "Superman's boring!
I've got a Batman cape."

I went back home.
My wicked stepmother said, "Hey, look! It's Superman,
come to rescue us from danger!"
I almost smiled at her but I didn't because she's my wicked
stepmother and I don't smile at wicked stepmothers.

I don't tell her what I think of her or she might turn me into a frog.

It was my birthday. Jack and David came to my party.
But in hot potato Jack cheated, and when we played musical
chairs, David pushed me off and I got mad and cried a lot.

Then the wicked stepmother

brought in the cake and it was like

a cat and had seven candles and I

lit them and took a deep breath.

But before I could blow them out,
Jack and David blew them out.
I was angry and started to cry.

The wicked stepmother said to David and Jack,
"If you do that again I'll turn you into nasty little toads!"

She lit the candles again and I blew them all out in one try.

And then we had presents and David gave me a toy car, and Jack gave me a toy car. Dad gave me two books and a tape and some new pajamas.

The wicked stepmother gave me a toy train set, which was what I really wanted. It was my favorite present, but I didn't play with it because it was bewitched.

Then my dad came home from work and David's mom and Jack's dad came to pick them up, and me and Dad read the storybooks he gave me and I put on my new pajamas and we had dinner and it was time to go to bed and Dad said . . .

. . . "Will you give Annie a kiss?" and I said, "No, I can't, she's a wicked stepmother and a horrible witch!" and then I thought, Oh no! Now she'll turn me into a toad!

But she didn't.

She cried.

I felt bad.

So I put my arms around her and kissed her, and she smiled and hugged me,

and I cried and Dad cried, and we all cried and hugged each other.

Then Dad took me up to bed and told me a story about a fairy godmother. And now I've discovered I must be a wizard —

because I used to have a wicked stepmother but I kissed her,
and now she's turned into a fairy godmother.